The Wild E... and the WILD WEST

CONTENTS

The Wild Easts

Written by Frances Bacon   Illustrated by Trevor Pye

For my mother, who also does yoga in the living room.

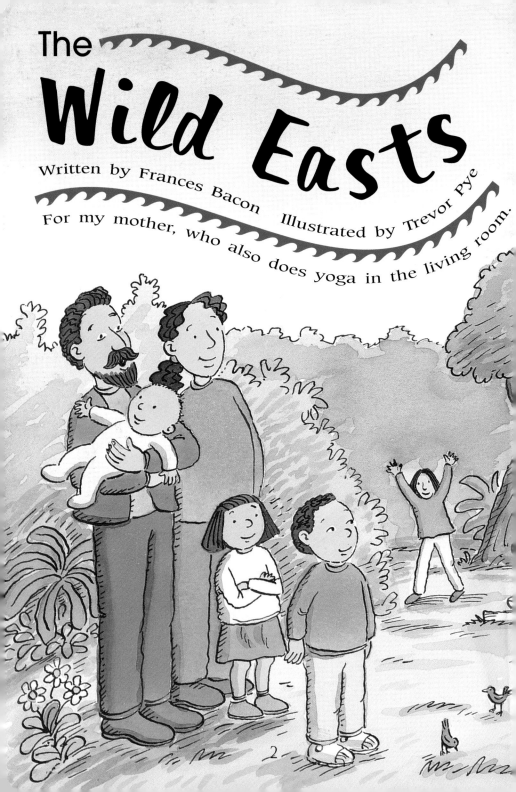

2

My brother and I went to stay
with our cousins, the Easts,
for a week. We had been looking
forward to our visit for a long time.

When our bus pulled
into the station, we saw a lot
of people waiting. All of them
were our cousins. There was Sky,
River, Daisy, Duke, and baby Zoë.

I said, "Hurray!"
My brother said,
"I want to go home."

7

When we arrived
at our cousins' house,
we couldn't believe our eyes.
The house was painted
with purple-and-yellow stripes,
the roof was green,
and the garden
had Wild West statues.

I said, "Wow!"
My brother said,
"I want to go home."

The inside of the house
was even stranger.
There were so many plants
that it looked like a jungle.
There were stairs
that led to nowhere,
and the kitchen was full
of science experiments.

I said, "Awesome!"
My brother said,
"I want to go home."

Dinner time was very unusual.
Instead of chairs,
we sat on saddles.
My cousins all wore cowboy hats.
Our serviettes were folded
into horseshoes.

I said, "Yeehah!"
My brother said,
"I want to go home."

When it came to bedtime,
we got another surprise.
There were no beds.
We all slept in hammocks.

I said, "Great!"
My brother said,
"I want to go home."

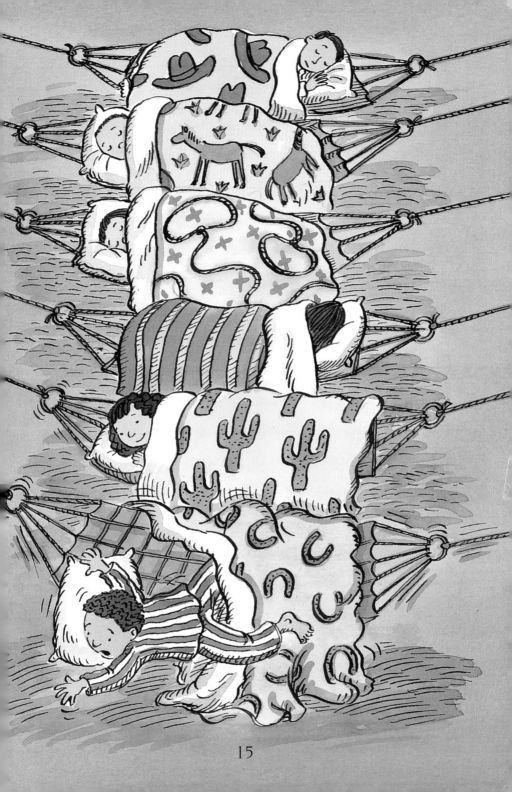

Each morning, Aunt Susan
woke us up very early.
"Time for our yoga," she said.
In the living room,
we all sat on mats.
My uncle stood on his head.

I said, "Cool!"
My brother said,
"I want to go home."

Next we helped
our cousins to feed the pets.
Instead of a cat, a dog, or even
a rabbit, they had pet snakes,
a kangaroo rat, and a Mexican
walking fish.

I said, "Amazing!"
My brother said,
"I want to go home."

In our cousins' garden,
they didn't have a tree house
with a rope ladder. They had
a tree castle with turrets,
a drawbridge, and a moat
full of snapping turtles!

I said, "Brilliant!"
My brother said,
"I want to go home."

21

Then Uncle Henry had to go
to work. Aunt Susan suggested
that we should all go with him.
He didn't work in a factory
or an office or a hospital.
Uncle Henry worked
at an amusement park.

I said, "Yahoo!"
My brother said,
"I *don't* want to go home, *not ever!*"

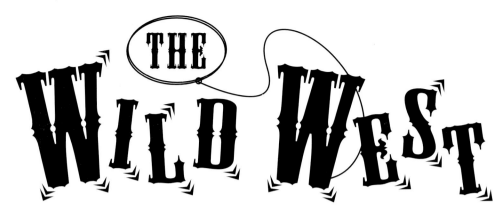

THE WILD WEST

Written by Janine Scott
Illustrated by Ian Forss

For my grandma,
the wildest sneezer in the West!

Way out in the desert,
where a wild wind blows
from the west, lived a wild
and woolly cowboy.

Yet he wasn't like other cowboys.
He sneezed and wheezed and
huffed and puffed all day long.
His horse made him sneeze.
His sheep made him sneeze.
Everything made him sneeze.

But his troubles really
began one gentle, mild morning.
As the grass whispered
in the wind and the wild flowers
blew in the breeze, the cowboy
went for a ride on his horse.

Then, all of a sudden,
the mild breeze turned
into a wild westerly wind.

Great clouds of dust swirled
and twirled around the cowboy.
"Ah-ah-ah-choo!" sneezed
the cowboy into his handkerchief.
The sneeze was so loud
that it sounded like a cracking
horsewhip.

His poor horse got such a fright that it ran off as fast as it could.

It ran faster than the tumbleweed.

It ran faster than a roadrunner.

It ran faster than stampeding cattle.

"Whoa, boy, whoa!"
cried the cowboy, trying his best
not to sneeze.

Suddenly, the sneezing cowboy
sneezed even louder than before,
and his horse ran even faster.

"Whoa, boy, whoa!" cried
the cowboy, as his horse jumped
over a fence into a rodeo.

"Yahoo!" yelled some cowboys.

"Yeehah!" yelled some cowgirls.

"Yippee! Look at that cowboy go!" cried a man with a microphone.

The horse kicked and jumped while the cowboy bounced and bumped. The cowboy didn't fall off though. He just held on tight.

Then the cowboy grabbed
his lasso and threw it. He aimed
it at a tree, but the lasso went
around a bull's legs instead.

To make things worse, the
cowboy sneezed again. (Bulls
made him sneeze!) The sneeze
blew the bull right off its feet.

Then the cowboy had an idea.
He wondered if he could jump
onto some bales of hay.
So he stood up on his saddle
and held onto the reins.

He rode around and around
the ring, but the horse never went
near the hay. It just bounced and
bumped and bucked the cowboy.
The cowboy still held on tight.

Finally, his horse got tired.
It slowed to a trot, then to a halt.

The next thing the cowboy knew, he was on the stage.

"Yahoo! You're the best bouncing, bumping, bucking buckaroo in the Wild West!" cried the man with the microphone.

The cowboy had won first prize for bull roping and bronco bucking. However, his troubles began again when the man gave him flowers.

"Ah-ah-ah-CHOO!" sneezed
the cowboy, and off he shot again.
He and his horse went on
to set a new rodeo time record
for the longest bronco bucking
in the West!

Finally, as the sun was setting in the Wild West, the cowboy stopped sneezing and his horse stopped bucking.

But then, as the grass whispered in the wind and the wild flowers blew in the breeze, a wild wind whipped in from the Wild East!

Ah-chooOOO!

Big families are great – you never get lonely and there is always a lot going on. So far, my daughters, Lucretia and Zoë, don't have any first cousins. But we do have other family members who make life wild!

Frances Bacon

I sneeze and wheeze and huff and puff like the sneezing cowboy. Luckily, I don't have a horse! But grass does the same thing to me. Uh-oh! I live in wild New Zealand – a country with lots of green, green grass... *Ah-ah-ah-choo*!

Janine Scott

FROM THE ILLUSTRATORS

 Like the boy in the story, I had only one sister, but I always wondered what it would be like having lots of brothers and sisters. I loved drawing *The Wild Easts*. It gave me an idea of life in a big, crazy family!

Trevor Pye

 A friend took me on my first horse ride. I climbed into the saddle and, whoosh, I was away. I tried to turn left and turn right. I cried, "Whoa!" But the horse just bolted ahead. Eventually, I jumped off. I got my revenge though. I married my friend!

Ian Forss